For my daughter, Mina

Due to choking hazards, boba is not recommended for children under 4.

Library of Congress Control Number 2020914830
ISBN 978-1-953281-04-3
Printed in Taiwan.

Visit **www.lycheepress.com**

I love BOBA!

Let's go and get some boba,

a drink **TAIWAN** created!

TAIWAN

It's loved by many people
and widely **CELEBRATED!**

But do you call it **BOBA**, pearl milk or bubble tea?
Whichever way you name it...

It's **DELICIOUS.**

You'll see!

Boba is the drink itself,
but here's something amusing.

They're also a sweet topping.
Same name, yes, it's confusing!

They look like **SHINY PEARLS**.
They're made of tapioca.

They're **SOAKED** in icy tea
or juice or sometimes mocha.

They come in many sizes,
from **LARGE** to small to *mini*.

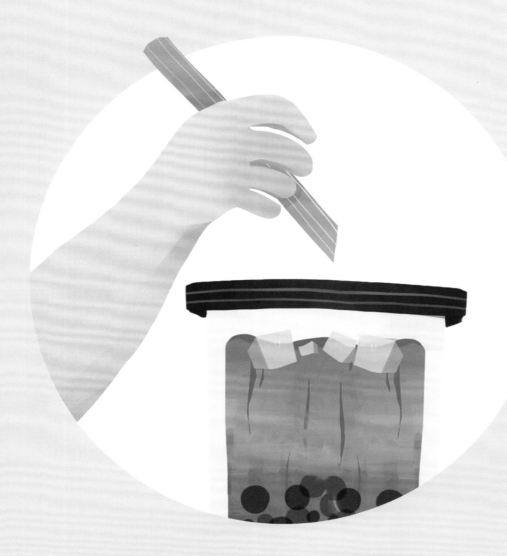

You'll need to use a **FAT** straw.
They'll clog in one that's *SKINNY!*

A **PERFECT** boba's chewy.
One taste will get you hooked!

They're too **HARD** when not cooked through,
too *SOFT* when overcooked.

Milk tea is a classic choice, but if you don't like dairy,

perhaps you should try matcha...

mango, melon, or berry!

Add on jellies, egg pudding,
red beans, or salted cheese!

There's even **POPPING** boba
that bursts juice with a squeeze!

All day, I DREAM of boba.
It's even gluten-free!

This beverage is AMAZING,
so try it! You'll agree!

CHEERS!!!